—Rosie's Christmas Eve

Susannah Bradley

Illustrated by Rebecca Archer

Hippo Books
Scholastic Publications Limited
London

Scholastic Publications Ltd.,
10 Earlham Street, London WC2H 9RX, UK

Scholastic Inc.,
730 Broadway, New York, NY 10003, USA

Scholastic Tab Publications Ltd.,
123 Newkirk Road, Richmond Hill,
Ontario L4C 3G5, Canada

Ashton Scholastic Pty. Ltd.,
P O Box 579, Gosford, New South Wales,
Australia

Ashton Scholastic Ltd., 165 Marua Road,
Panmure, Auckland 6, New Zealand

Published by Scholastic Publications Ltd., 1990
Text copyright © Susannah Bradley, 1990.
Illustrations copyright © Rebecca Archer, 1990

ISBN 0 590 76359 8
All rights reserved

Made and printed in Spain by Mateu Cromo, Madrid.

10 9 8 7 6 5 4 3 2 1

"Horrible old Christmas Eve," said Rosie.
"Horrible old Father Christmas."

"What's the matter, Rosie?" asked Mum.
"It's Christmas Eve and he hasn't come,"
said Rosie. "Father Christmas has forgotten
all about me."

"It's not time for him to come yet," said
Mum. "Come and help me ice the cake."

"Now where did I put the little Father Christmas for the top of the cake?" said Mum.

"But I don't know why he is taking so long to come," said Rosie after lunch. "When I saw him at the playschool party he had his red suit on, all ready. And that was days ago."

"Ah, but he still had to get all the toys ready. And he has to deliver them around the world, Rosie," said Mum. "I've got some presents to wrap up, too. Would you like to help me?"

"Which parcel has got Dad's new cricket
bat in it?" asked Rosie.

"Father Christmas gave me a jigsaw at the playschool party," said Rosie. "Maybe he won't bring me anything else."

"Of course he will," said Mum. "Come upstairs with me and help me find a stocking for you to hang up."

"Somewhere I have a pair of long socks
with spots on. Can you see a sock like that,
Rosie?"

"But what if Father Christmas forgets where
I live?" asked Rosie.

"He won't forget," said Mum. "You sent him a letter, didn't you? But we can prop this card up in your bedroom window anyway, so that he will see it as he drives along in his sleigh tonight."

"We must keep the cat out of here, or he
may knock the card down," said Mum.

"Freddy, where are you?" called Rosie.

"But he won't see our Christmas tree lights because Dad hasn't got our tree yet," said Rosie.

"Hello!" called Dad. "Is there anyone in this house who could help me decorate a Christmas tree?"

"Me, me!" shouted Rosie. "Let me help!"

They had a lovely time decorating the tree.
"Isn't there a fairy to go on the top,
Rosie?" asked Dad.

"Everything's ready for Christmas now,"
said Rosie. "But what if Father Christmas
forgets that it is Christmas Eve tonight?"

"He can't do that," said Mum. "The angels
will be singing Christmas carols!"
"I think I can hear them now," said Dad.

But it was a group of carol singers with a collecting tin.

"Lovely!" said Mum. "I've got some coins
here somewhere, which you can have."

"Time for bed," said Mum.

"But I'm not sleepy," said Rosie. "If I can't go to sleep, Father Christmas won't come, will he?"

"Wait until you've had this nice warm drink,
and then see how sleepy you are," said
Dad.

"Where's your bear?" asked Dad.
     "Oh, Rosie," said Mum. "There's such a bright star in the sky!"

"That's the Christmas star!" cried Rosie.
"Now I know that everything's going to be
all right!"